Beech Farm

Walter's Garage

Mallard Pond

Idwood Brook

For Kerrie—C.R.

Text copyright © 1990 by Elizabeth Laird
Illustrations and characters copyright © 1990 by
Colin Reeder
First published in Great Britain
by William Collins Sons & Co. Ltd.

Tambourine Books,
a division of William Morrow & Company, Inc.,
105 Madison Avenue, New York, New York 10016.

Library of Congress Cataloging in Publication Data
Laird, Elizabeth. The day Patch stood guard / by Elizabeth Laird ;
pictures by Colin Reeder.   p.   cm.—(A little red tractor book)
Summary: Patch, a young sheepdog, becomes a guard dog when
farmer Stan's little red tractor, Duncan, has an accident.
ISBN 0-688-10239-5 (trade)—ISBN 0-688-10240-9 (lib.)
[1. Dogs—Fiction. 2. Tractors—Fiction. 3. Farms—Fiction.]
I. Reeder, Colin, ill.   II. Title.   III. Series.
PZ7.L1579Dax   1991 [E]—dc20   90-11153 CIP AC
Printed in Portugal
First U.S. edition 1991
1   3   5   7   9   10   8   6   4   2

A Little Red Tractor Book

The Day
Patch Stood Guard

ELIZABETH LAIRD

pictures by COLIN REEDER

TAMBOURINE BOOKS · NEW YORK

A blackbird was singing loudly one bright May morning on Gosling Farm, but Stan the farmer didn't hear him. He was fast asleep.

A fly buzzed around his nose. Stan turned over and went on snoring. A paw scratched at his bedroom door. Patch, the young dog, wanted her breakfast.

Stan woke up with a jerk. He looked at his clock. It had stopped in the night. Stan jumped out of bed. "Oh, my goodness, I've overslept!" he said. "And there are the cows to milk, and the pigs to feed, and the eggs to collect and . . . All right, Patch, I'm coming!"

Stan dressed quickly and hurried off to do the milking. Patch ran out after him. The farmyard was full of exciting smells. Patch pushed her wet nose under a door. It bumped a bigger, wetter nose on the other side. A calf was sniffing the spring air too.

Patch jumped back and licked her nose clean. A butterfly floated above her head. Patch jumped after it. It fluttered across to Duncan, the little red tractor. Patch liked Duncan. She curled up against his rear wheel and waited for Stan.

The sun was already high when Stan was finished with the milking.
He hitched up the trailer and piled some lumber into it.

"Come on, Duncan," he said. "We've got to get down to the brook
and mend the old bridge. Some of those planks are rotten through."

He climbed into Duncan's cab, and Patch scrambled up after him.
Then Duncan rumbled out of the barn and down the road.

The lambs were happy to see the little red tractor. They jumped about on their long thin legs and bleated at him.

Patch stood up. She was a sheepdog. She knew about lambs. She'd watched her mother round them up and bring them to the farmer. She'd show Stan that she could do it too. She jumped out of the cab.

"Hey! Patch! Careful, girl!" shouted Stan as he climbed out after her.

Patch lay down in the grass and put her long nose on her paws. She watched Stan, ready to obey his orders. She wouldn't move a whisker until he told her to.

"Here! Patch!" called Stan.

Patch jumped up and ran to him. Stan was pleased. Patch was a sheepdog, born and bred. He could trust her not to chase the lambs after all. He turned back to Duncan.

Then Stan got a dreadful fright. He
had left Duncan's handbrake off, and
the little red tractor was rolling down
the hill out of control. Stan started
running after him. "The brook!" wailed
Stan. "He's going to end up in the
brook! No, he's not, he's going to crash
through the fence! No, he's not, he's
going to hit the tree!" With a bump,
Duncan hit the tree.

The little tractor was in a sorry state. Oil dripped from his brake pipe. His front grill was bent, and his headlights were broken. The trailer had come off and turned over on its side. Curious lambs crowded round to look at him. "Oh, dear," said Stan, shaking his head. "This is a job for Walter, up at the garage.

"Here, Patch, you stay and guard poor old Duncan while I go phone Walter," said Stan.

Patch wagged her tail and sat down by Duncan's rear wheel. She looked fierce. She'd guard Duncan all right, no question of that.

It was a long time before Stan came back with Walter. Patch was very glad to see him. She barked with joy.

Walter inspected the trailer.

"There's not much wrong with this," he said. "You can nail those boards back yourself."

Then he looked at Duncan. This time, he shook his head.

"Hmm," he said. "I can't work on him here. We'll have to hitch him to the tow truck and take him back to the garage."

So Walter and Stan hooked Duncan up to the truck and they set off.

In the garage, Stan drove Duncan onto a ramp, and Walter pressed a button. The little red tractor rose into the air.

Walter peered carefully into Duncan's insides. Then he lowered Duncan down to the ground again.

"It's not too bad," he said. "Leave him here tonight, Stan, and I'll work on him tomorrow. He should be fine by the afternoon."

The two men went on talking as they left the garage. Patch sat down beside Duncan. Stan had told her to guard the little red tractor, and she was going to do just that.

Five minutes passed, then ten. Patch heard a car starting up outside the garage. Walter was taking Stan home! They'd been so worried about Duncan they'd forgotten all about her!

It was getting dark. Patch was scared. She wanted to go home. She scrambled up into Duncan's cab. She felt better there. Duncan was an old friend.

A long time later, the garage door opened. Walter came in. "Patch!" he said, "Stan's worried sick about you. He's just called me. I promised I'd take you home."

He tried to pick Patch up, but she growled at him. Stan had told her to guard Duncan, and no one was going to stop her. Walter laughed. "All right, you win," he said. "Stan will take you home tomorrow."

Walter brought Patch a big bowl of supper and some water. She ate everything up, then settled down in Duncan's cab and fell fast asleep.

The next day Walter drove Duncan out into the sunny garage yard. He unscrewed the broken bits, bolted on the new bits, and soon Duncan was as good as new.

   Patch lay in the sun with her ears cocked and watched Walter carefully. She was still on guard.

At last, Stan arrived. Patch was overjoyed. She wagged her tail so hard that her back half wagged with it. Walter laughed at her.

"She's the best little guard dog I ever did see," he said.

Later, Stan drove Duncan up the road that led to Gosling Farm. He hadn't forgotten Patch this time. Her nose was poking out of the tractor's window. Patch's sharp eyes spotted something. A sleek, dark head with a fine set of whiskers was swimming downstream through the clear, clean water. "The otter," said Stan quietly. Patch nearly barked, but Stan laid his hand on her head. "Quiet, girl," he said, "We don't want to frighten him."

The otter dived down into the brook, and only a ripple showed where he had been. Stan turned Duncan and drove him up the road toward the farmyard. The sun sparkled on Duncan's new grill and shimmered on his bright new headlights. As Duncan passed Five Oaks Pasture, the lambs frisked over to their gate to watch him rumble by. The mother goose, leading her goslings down to the brook, stretched out her long neck and cackled at him. Everyone was glad to see the little red tractor home safe again.

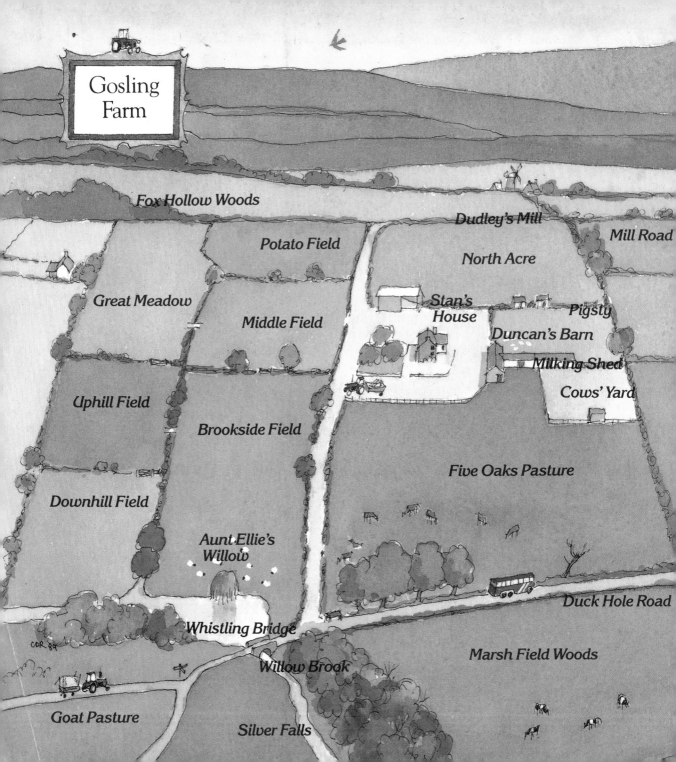

Gosling
Farm

Fox Hollow Woods

Dudley's Mill

Mill Road

Potato Field

North Acre

Great Meadow

Stan's
House

Pigsty

Middle Field

Duncan's Barn

Milking Shed

Uphill Field

Cows' Yard

Brookside Field

Five Oaks Pasture

Downhill Field

Aunt Ellie's
Willow

Duck Hole Road

Whistling Bridge

Marsh Field Woods

Willow Brook

Goat Pasture

Silver Falls

COR 89